ROT

Janet Kauffman

New Issues Poetry & Prose

A Green Rose Book
Selected by Jaimy Gordon

New Issues Poetry & Prose
Western Michigan University
Kalamazoo, Michigan 49008

An Inland Seas Book

 Inland Seas books are supported by a grant from
The Michigan Council for Arts and Cultural Affairs.

First Edition, 2001.

ISBN: 1-930974-02-7 (paperbound)

Library of Congress Cataloging-in-Publication Data:
Kauffman, Janet
Rot/Janet Kauffman
Library of Congress Catalog Card Number (00-132522)

Art Direction and Design: Tricia Hennessy
Production: Paul Sizer
                             The Design Center,
                             Department of Art
                             College of Fine Arts
                             Western Michigan University
Printing: Courier Corporation

ROT

Janet Kauffman

New Issues

WESTERN MICHIGAN UNIVERSITY

Also by Janet Kauffman

One section of *Rot* appeared
in slightly different form,
as the story "Sour" in *Witness*.

Contents

"People were a lot more honest
and emotional in those days.
If they didn't like the way it was,
they shot themselves."
        —Svetlana Alliluyeva,
            Stalin's daughter,
            20 Letters to a Friend

1

Stalin Never Caught Up With My Father

My father, unlike Stalin, will not walk into a dream and break my arm, the snap so loud it wakes me.

Stalin has kicked and crushed the bones of my legs. Thrown me into a mud ditch. Dead himself, he has more than once pulled out a shovel, brought it down on my skull, and buried me alive.

My father does not have a mustache. He shaves before breakfast, and he is a pacifist—look at the gentleness of his legs, his thighs limber and his feet in slippers. He's alive, with a book in his lap, *Scenes from the Life of Stalin*. Stalin was dead before I could read.

One day in summer when I was a girl, my father appeared to me to be born. It's the first memory I have, and what else can you call the beginning of life?

It is late summer, it must be: we're cutting tobacco, hanging it in the tobacco shed—green leaves fill the peak overhead. Memory has peculiar containments, roofs without edge or frame.

It's dark and my father lands at my feet. He arrives feet first, and I see the brown shoes, the work clothes, the white shirt sleeves, and finally his face in the shadow of his cap. In memory, the motion is fluid, a man assembling himself out of darkness, a planet coming into view and shaping itself into a body.

He climbed down, out of air blurred with tobacco dust, carrying with him the black and green light from the peak of the shed. I saw the soles of his work shoes, then the bend of his knees. He balanced a foot on one beam, a hand on another, then he swung himself down to the barn floor, took off his cap and wiped his face.

There he was. And is. One day there is nothing; and the next, everything—everything you can imagine. And what, after all, is unimaginable?

———————————

There was a time men lived in their mothers' laps. Even grown, they lived and died there, and called them rolling fields, hollows, swales, plains. They fought there, arm to arm, thigh across thigh, the way they fought at Gettysburg. They spoke their mother's tongue.

As a boy and as a man, Jesus rested in Mary's arms. He slept there, slumped. He raised his hand and spoke there. Look at the folds of lap cloth and draped head cloth. He didn't fight. In Pennsylvania, the Mennonite women held sleeping boys, see the dark fabrics, arm across arm, hand to hand. Plain as plain. Nobody fought.

With field enough, there is no end to plain.

With fabric enough, there is no end to folding, overlapping.

And with words, just try to say no, try to say, no, it is not my mother's tongue.

Stalin never caught up with my father. Although, not long before my father was born, Stalin was already writing pamphlets, talking up socialism with the tobacco farmers of Tiflis. He was still Joseph Djugashvili, still Koba, living with his mother.

He squatted there at the edges of tobacco fields, picked at stray leaves, stripped them down to the stem, squeezed the juice out of the stalk, and rubbed at the tar on his hands. Stalin loved the smell of tobacco and so did Svetlana, his daughter. Their apartment, years later in the Kremlin, like a tobacconist's shop, held the scent of Stalin's cigars. Even though the rooms were nearly empty, and nearly the same, each one with a chair, a table, a sofa, nothing more than that—each room a hut to itself. The air that filled those rooms was the air of long-leaved Georgian tobacco, cured in dark sheds my father knew, top to bottom.

I have never dreamed about my father. My mother—she's dead but that doesn't stop her—is the one who meets me and travels around with me in dream. We talk and we ride in silent cars; we fly over Svetlana's apartment; we open the door of a warehouse—it's the same as daily living. My mother wants to buy celery and we drive to the celery farm. On a routine flight to Cuba, the airplane ditches in Havana harbor and, as the plane sinks, my mother opens the window by my seat and says, There you go. She pushes me out. She is very young and wears a red silk dress she would never have worn.

When my father was young he would not have tolerated the aimless travel in dream. But now that he's old, and aimlessness has its virtues, maybe some night he'll show up. Walk through a door without opening it, wearing velvet, which he would never wear.

He's not a man for entertainments. He won't turn on the T. V. At breakfast, he reads the newspaper. He'll read biographies; but he won't read fiction, not even this, where I make him up and sit him at the window.

These last few weeks, my father has read biographies of Hitler and Mussolini. Jim Jones. He's re-reading books about Stalin. This morning he says, Listen to this. He reads me the story of Stalin and his bodyguard, whose wife has given him fur-lined felt slippers so that, as bodyguard, he can move through Stalin's room at night, *unheard*. She would not have Stalin disturbed.

"You can move about the apartment unheard?" Stalin asks.

"Yes," says the bodyguard.

"You can move about my room unheard? Unheard?"

Well, what can you say, what can you say, my father says. You say yes to Stalin, you say no, you're a dead man. The fact is, you have to watch every word. And that's impossible.

At Stalin's death, Svetlana discovered her father's drawings of wolves. "I had no idea," she said. She claimed that Stalin's sketches of wolf heads and wolf bodies in the margins of state papers, his drawings of wolf tracks between the lines of signatories—she called them doodles among scribblings—meant nothing to no one.

"The double negative," Irene Iruskaiya said. "Watch out. *Nothing to no one* in English means: *something to everyone.*"

They sat in fog on the beach at Cape May, Svetlana and Irene Iruskaiya, my father's new friend—he calls her I., for short, like somebody in a red scarf in a novel.

Old women, toned legs, in black bathing suits. Irene with a red scarf tied in her hair. The fog shifted around them like water, their blanket a flashy purple and green raft.

"No, you know what I mean," Svetlana said. "They were leftovers, worthless."

"But," I. said, "when Stalin was doodling these wolf leftovers in a meeting, you don't think Malenkov or whoever that day sat at his right hand ignored his scribblings?"

Svetlana kicked out one leg and looked off through the fog.

The edge of the water, the last run of foam up the wet sand, dropped a pink shell like a fingernail near her toes. "No, it's true," she said, "nobody ignored Papa. But he hid so much. He could write in the crook of his elbow, his arm curled around the paper, you know, and no one could read. I never saw his wolves, and they were all over household lists. When he died, I found papers and papers, these wolf heads, in the kitchen drawer and they were like strangers to me."

"Like me, a stranger?" I. said.

"Sure! Another sheet of paper in the desk, who knows! That's you, Irene Iruskaiya. What do we know of things not shaped by our own hands? The knife is a stranger to me until I pick it up."

"And cut into something?" I. said.

"Like meat."

"And take a fork?" I. said.

"Sure, pull back the muscle."

"Eat it?"

"Flesh is no stranger now!" Svetlana said.

Strangers, they talked all weekend at the beach, argued, but stuck with each other and stayed up late drinking Turkish coffee in paper cups. They walked out onto the slabs of the breakwater and sat there in the dark.

"We are so far from everything," Svetlana said.

"Not me," Irene Iruskaiya said. "I was born in New Jersey."

"But your father," Svetlana said. She pushed her hands out in the dark. "Your family. All the past?"

"It's not the same."

"A father's a father," Svetlana insisted.

"You're a foolish woman," I. said. "You want to die foolish?"

"And what do you know about anything?" Svetlana said. She crumpled the paper cup in her hand, threw it into the wet sand between rocks. "New Jersey! You with no past to be far off from. Your father, such a good man, I'm sure, dead as anybody and not spoken of any more. Well, fine. Who *are* you sitting out here, so empty?"

There's the well-known episode when Stalin threw bread pellets at his wife. She was such an idealist.

Not that bread, even in pellets, or Stalin-size handfuls of crumbs, or wheat flour dust, whatever the shape of peasant policy, could kill her.

Nadya, mother of Svetlana, shot herself.

At a party, she said what she had to say about Stalin's collectivization policies, ensuing famine, all those things, and there was bread at this party of course which Stalin picked up and threw at her, along with other obscenities.

Strange to see him so close up. His hands pulling the bread apart. The wool of the sleeve. One arm drawing back. The vodka twisting him around, his lips still open, the laugh just shutting down. His left eyebrow, that giveaway arch. He is familiar. Horrible. Uncle Someone.

Nadya in her black silk evening dress. She'd studied textiles, the engineering of viscose products, at the All-Union Industrial Academy. Nadya loved silk, and she was young. She could imagine, she could *invent*, fabrics as soft as silk, but affordable, bolts in the warehouses of all the towns, spun and woven. Like straw into gold, she is said to have said.

"No one cannot buy straw," Svetlana said to I. "Right? *Everyone* can! Straw into gold. Bread pellets on silk. That's Russian."

Svetlana said when she defected, she flew out with nothing but her own clothes. She had nothing of her mother's.

Her mother had so little anyway. She did have that gun. She knew from the early days how to use it, and she was fearless. Talking to Stalin that way. Talking to her husband Stalin. Who threw bread pellets at her, and mocked her in Georgian and in Russian. Nadya was small, with thin, strong arms and very dark hair. She smoothed the black silk of her dress, turned, and went home. In the apartment, she hung up her coat; she brushed and smoothed out the skirt of her dress. And stood there. And took the necessary steps—into the bedroom, to the bureau for the gun. She took the three steps back to see the silk dress in the mirror, the flexed arm aiming the gun.

———————————————

Irene Iruskaiya told my father about Stalin's wolf drawings. Last year, he was on the boardwalk at Cape May with his binoculars and a fat biography of Duvalier. She sat down beside him.

"You can watch birds and read at the same time?" she asked, as introduction.

Alternately, he said.

This is how I. picked up people. In her old age, she liked to snag them. Not necessarily bring them together—my father never met Svetlana, never felt he was close to meeting her. That was another year. Svetlana had visited the shore just once, and was not suited to basking, I. said, not in New Jersey. She needed the limelight.

Did you see any of the drawings? my father asked. He coughed and leaned over. Irene Iruskaiya made two fists and rubbed between his shoulder blades.

I do some drawing, my father said. Leaves. Tobacco leaves. Tree bark. A bit of it. It's not easy drawing dry leaves. I'm not very good at it.

"Tree bark?" I. said.

It's all different. Individual, my father said. Like faces, except that it stands still. You can stare and memorize it.

14

"Well, I didn't see any wolf drawings," I. said. "He must have made up the wolves, don't you think? He couldn't have seen wolves much, or stared at them."

Invented wolves, imagined wolves, my father said. Yes. He was Stalin, after all. He's not a man to draw dry leaves.

Tobacco's but an Indian Weed,
Grows Green in the Morn, cut down at Eve . . .

My father sings a line or two of the song. I don't think he knows the words all the way through. He never sings any song to the end, just a phrase or two, the main melody line, and sometimes I think he's made these up, they aren't well-known songs, not any of them.

Tobacco, he sings, to a bluesier tune, it's a goddamn beauty.

The lines about tobacco—Elizabethan, or Southern, or Mennonite farm songs, who knows—they're all his, and I've heard them since I was old enough to drive the tractor, maybe I was eight or nine, and he loaded the laths of tobacco onto the wagon behind me, whistling these tunes, or mouthing the words at me when I looked back, braking for the next heap of stalks. My cousin Randolph walked along beside the wagon and when I braked, he lifted the laths with five stalks speared onto each one—green skirts speared on sticks. My father hung them up. It took a minute, and then I sat down on the tractor seat and let up the brake pedal and we rolled to the next stack of laths and wilted leaves.

That was the after-school routine for me in September: drive to the field, pick up my father at the end of a row—just slow down for him to swing himself onto the wagon—slow more for the first heap of stalks, stand on the brake so my full weight could hold the stop, sit down and raise the pedal, drive ahead in the dust, stand up, sit down, second gear, that's all there was to it. But the facts of the work I hardly remember; I've had to re-set my feet through the motions to recall. What remains, no trouble to remember, none— it is what I think of as memory—is the air there, the dust (airborne particles, fine). The clay and tobacco grit, the sticker sun, smear of tobacco tar on the steering wheel, and the dirt I licked off my arms. The smell of spit, and sun all over the new muscle of my own forearm. I licked it and sucked it. A girl sung to. My father mouthed bits of sound in the air, in the whirlwinds, leaf-lolling. His words winding forward through air, through my hair to the bowls and hollows of my ears, ears shaped exactly like his. We were in it together, those days.

I could have, and would have, said he was my mother.

Look what a rich man pays for Havana cigars, he sang after the embargo. Oh, look how they smuggle them in.

That was a new tune, the old theme. By the time I left high school, I'd had my political training. He never used the words class or exploitation or anything but rich and poor. But attached to tobacco and cigars, those words added up.

Tobacco's just what it always was, a rich man's start and a poor man's end—he hummed the rest—or was it, a poor man's start and a rich man's end? He probably sang both. My father found paradox always to the point. Contradiction made sure sense. This-equals-that, no matter the terms, was his idea of poetry, and he spouted political equations: Lancaster County, hey, it's Cuba. Tobacco leaves are dollar bills, green and gold.

The tobacco brokers from Lancaster came around to the fields sometimes, and they had a different take on tobacco, a licentious line, even with Mennonites. One of the brokers had a way of handling the leaves, looking them over, pressing out the velvet sheen of them, and saying, "Touch that, touch that. Look at that beauty."

It wasn't my father's goddamn beauty.

One summer the broker said it out loud, "The tobacco leaf should be shaped like a woman, n'est-ce pas?"

But a cigar, she's so manly, my father replied.

These were the facts of life: smoking was sin, and tobacco, the money crop.

The good life was so much sing-song.

I tell my father now, I'm thankful for it, the knowledge at an early age: nothing is pure and simple. Not nature, human or otherwise. There is no pure reason. No simple situation or character. No pure thought, or feeling, or logic. No simple action. No good work.

We are compromised utterly.

Still, my father says—he looks up from Svetlana's account of her father—you have to know what's what. Draw conclusions. You can't let anybody off the hook.

He means the daughter's on the hook as well as the father. He means pure or not, one thing leads to another.

One thing does lead to another:

A good man, a pacifist, sees brutality in himself as well as in brutal men. Therefore, a good man cannot be good. Therefore, a good man must watch himself closely, every move. Therefore, a good man slows his pace, stalks the tyrant he knows is himself. Therefore, the good man, and not the tyrant, identifies with the tyrant.

The good man draws conclusions, and soon he, too, is drawing Stalin's wolves.

Like anybody else, my father has breathed air all his life. And he's breathed in tobacco dust, alfalfa hay dust, the powdery field dusts.

"It's green lung," Irene tells him.

But it has a more ordinary name. Lung cancer. Complicated now with throat cancer. He refuses surgery, he believes it is too violent, and too late. No, he says, I've got a scar.

And he does, like a piece of string on the front of his neck.

It's not going to happen again, he says. Nobody's going to cut my throat.

I make dinner for my father: chicken corn soup, blended and sieved. He soaks bread in it and swallows carefully.

He says, This tastes good.

He leans over the book by his plate and reads: Stalin's threat to reduce a jailor by a head, if he didn't get a confession from a prisoner, was in fact carried out.

Reduced by a head, my father says.

My father had his throat cut, before he moved in with me. The surgeon removed a chunk of his thyroid, a lump the size of plum. My father couldn't speak for a few weeks, and when he did his voice had a musical vibration to it, something like a kazoo. While he was silent, during the time words wouldn't appear or exit in the shape he wanted, he sat at the table and began his sketches.

My father's long scar, red at first and now pearly, lies where a necklace would lie on a woman.

The kazoo-ness of his talk disappeared; but my father's voice is thin, with an aluminum rattle to it. He doesn't mind. He says he couldn't use a voice of command. He couldn't stand to hear it.

If my father talks too long, his voice falls apart, into whispered phrases. From across a table, his words often hum, unrecognizable. Irene leans close, they go head to head, hushed, in a conversation.

From the other side of a field, my father's voice drops to nothing, and if he flails his arms like a person sending a message, Irene yells, "Cut!" and gives him the cut-the-throat sign so he'll wait there with what he has on his mind until she can walk across.

There was a time in the cultivation of Paradise, seven miles east of Lancaster, that tobacco flourished in the low fields. It grew leafy from soils fine as powder, washed and sieved between two rivers, where nothing else grew. The tobacco leaves rose and spread out, large as aprons or kites, a cloth of soft hairs, and the hand lingered and stroked the leaves—that was farming.

By the time the tobacco plant flowered, its stalk had become woody, and the fields between the two rivers were fields of tobacco trees, exactly the height of a human head.

Some mistakes were made in this place, including the naming of trees. That tree, the forbidden one, of the knowledge of good and evil, for instance. It was not the apple. Apples were eaten day after day, there was nothing forbidden about them. Fruit trees hid nothing from humans—they were wholly and fully known, grafted, with an understanding, from day one, of apple cider and schnitz and pie and cake.

But tobacco, which was nameless then, that was the tree-thing tobacco worms riddled, fumed about. Nobody knew better then. But then, they knew.

The knowledge of good and evil, all in one. Both. Somebody finally said, I know my own mind.

And after that, knowing what they knew, memory, like the landscape, lost its simple-mindedness, its idyll, its clear-cut narration. There was no big picture. Fields, wetlands, cities, and forests webbed with each other, mixes of matters overlapped, one place was no better than another, and about time.

Memory became like dream, complex and real, with blanknesses in it as well as soaking sunlight, and lulls, knife-fights, and unaccountable lapses.

Once in a while, though, even now, when a plant—any plant at all—startles with its panicled flower or elaborate leaf, notice how a person stops, looks off, and there it is, what we know cannot be dream and cannot be real, because it is so clear: the no-place tobacco flourishes without purpose, unscrolls its leaves over red ground, a set-aside place for touch, for peace-making, and for watching through days the summer-long sprawl of greenery.

———————————

In his chair by the window, my father sketches leaves. I tell him last night's dream: Stalin walks down the gravel road, swinging a chain, and from this chain hangs a severed head, noosed.

My father flips back a few pages in his sketchbook. He finds one of his drawings of me, my head and eyeballs and hair:

And in one of those moves that reminds you of dream, he turns the page upside-down, draws a few lines, and says, Here, was it this?

I couldn't say. It hadn't crossed my mind.

But my father drew the line, crossed it, and now I'd have to say what crosses his mind crosses mine. When I think of *him*, I think of *me*. And Irene—what can I do?—he calls her I.! When he mentions her, says what she says, how can I, or anybody, not think of him, and me? She, we.

We're a triumvirate: a trinity with no son, no ghost. There's father, daughter, hovering I. A Fatherhead—outnumbered by women, 2 to 1!

Fog closes in at the windows. There's a dispersal of light and damp, even on the skin. My father moves to the kitchen table. He presses the hair, soft and pale, on his arms, he irons it towards his wrists. Around him, he arranges paper, a couple of his pens. He opens his cardboard box of dried tobacco leaves—in this weather, the leaves aren't brittle. My father lifts them out, six or seven of them, separates them, and sets one aside to sketch.

That's how he does it. A leaf, like a shoe, in space. Dark edged, dark veined. Wrinkled, but not withered.

Black and white, the leaves aren't real. They don't command background, they're long gone from greenery. They're tobacco leaves that aren't tobacco. Fields, warehouses, cigars—they're somewhere. Not here. The lines on paper, like words, set apart leaf from everything else. There's nothing to them. They don't need stalk, root, stem, or dirt, and look around, everybody's shoes on the floor, they don't have them.

2

My Father Thinks Irene Might Shoot Him

Irene Iruskaiya, by her own account, is a liar, a shoplifter, an infiltrator, a rat. She is not a good person—she says she has no decency because it's an obstacle to thought.

Even so, Irene is a good friend to my father. She bought a house in a subdivision over the hill, and in good weather, they meet half-way at the ash tree, and walk three miles around the cul-de-sacs, circle drives, half loops with no sidewalks.

Irene encourages trespass. She takes my father's hand and pulls him onto front yards. She's pointed out their footpath to me, like a deer path meandering through private property, avoiding roadways, rounding the angles off corners. Irene loves the New Jersey shore, it's her native place; and a couple of times, May through October, she calls up my father, lures him away on vacation, lures me. She carries my father's books to any beach. They talk about evil, compare notes, and watch the dolphins offshore. He sketches her scarves, her knuckles. He sketches her face, forehead to chin. It's a perfect oval, he says.

What's a perfect oval? I ask him. What's the equation?

Well, symmetrical, then, he says. It's a perfectly symmetrical face.

Irene plucks her eyebrows and re-draws them, swayback Romanesque arches. She plucks her hairline. But otherwise, she lets her hair go wild, unclipped, unstyled. Her hair is so long now that when my father takes her hand, he sometimes holds her black hair in his hand, too. When she walks out of the ocean, drenched, her hair falls almost to her knees, like a poncho. If she's walking in an onshore wind, she'll pull out the red scarf from her sack and tie her hair down at her waist. Her hair is a hood, a wrap, a disguise.

You can see why she might get away with murder.

_____

I don't worry about my father. He and Irene are in cahoots, and it's something like spying. They whisper. They follow people, they report back. They touch each other on the arm and communicate without speaking. They track whatever is making tracks. She wears him out, but when I caution him on that, he says, Thank god.

He tells me that, like a Mennonite joining the old church, he's turning plain, for the end of his life. He will turn plainer and more plain, and then he will disappear. He wants to do nothing. Nothing important, nothing of consequence.

Purposelessness is next to godliness, he writes on a page of leaves. And he passes the sketchbook across the table for me to see.

Irene stands behind him and pets his hair. She's an accomplice to his drawing, his doing-of-nothing these days. An accompanist. She touches him on the shoulder, she blows at the hair around his ear. My father has such fine hair, Irene uses the word *silken* and she is right. His hair looks casual, careless. A contradiction to his arms, which are narrow, hard carved things, a twist of muscle down to the wrist from the motions of fieldwork.

"How can you not love that phrase," Irene says, "*manual labor?*" She drags her fingers like disks down the back of his hand.

Sometimes when he sketches a tobacco leaf, just a solitary leaf, Irene says to him, "Draw your hand, too."

And that's the whole page: the leaf on top; under it, the skeletal back of his hand.

You can see how she sees. She'll point to a couple of things and say, "Now that adds up."

My father says, I could listen to her all day.

One of Irene's ideas is this: There are two environments for tyranny: here and there; inside and out.

"The lines, of course, blur," Irene says. "Look how Svetlana, Stalin's daughter, struggled, because she could not torment herself."

Would not, my father says.

Did not, I say.

Svetlana could have dirtied her hair and boiled celery for soup. She could have plucked her eyebrows. She could have kept her name, Svetlana Alliluyeva. Or taken Stalin's. Svetlana Stalina. She could have said: I am not a good daughter of Stalin. Or, with her plucked brows: Yes, look at me, I am the daughter of Stalin.

But no. She believed she was, what else?, a daughter of a father! She believed she could travel, depart, defect, return. Or furnish a house and buy a Ford. She flew into JFK, she held a press conference at the Plaza. Without attaching herself to anybody in particular, combing her blonded hair, she said, I'm a daughter, we're all sons and daughters, I'm a daughter.

And a wife. In America, she took her husband's name and changed her own. Lana.

Lana Peters, listen to it. Russia's long gone.

Lana, such a swing to that skirt. A starlet.

When the marriage soured, it was cinematic, no doubt, the play-out of the scene: Lana Peters turns, walks out the door, with a good slam to it—she kicks the door shut with her high heel.

Think of the work, to come and go, so clean.

Irene Iruskaiya plays dirty. "If I get caught, I get caught," she says. She mumbles.

What? my father asks.

Irene says she's never bought one stick of the dark brown eyeliner she uses. Not one.

You steal? my father asks.

"I take it," I. says. "Because I pay for everything else. I always pay."

---

3 *Examples of How Irene Plays Dirty: #1*

She walks my father off the beach, across the boardwalk, into the Rite Aid drugstore. My father tells me the details: how, one hand in his, she leads him down the aisle to the Maybelline pencils, picks the dark brown pencil off a hook, splits the packet apart, cardboard from clear plastic, one-handed—her fingernail chisels the seal open—and slipping the pencil into her palm, she sets the empty package on the soap shelf. Then she picks up some soaps, she sets them down. She browses, selects an expensive hand lotion, and taking my father's arm, she makes her way to the checkout express, and pays in cash.

Back on the boardwalk, in bright sun, without a mirror, Irene takes the pencil and lines her eyes—she smears the corners with her fingertip, pulls the dark line out and up.

"If they catch me, they catch me," she says.

My father looks at her eyes and laughs. Then he takes the pencil and, as steady as he can, lines his own eyes.

Their faces both look pale. They look like they need sun. Like they need makeup.

Example #2:

When Irene Iruskaiya and my father walk, she carries a thick Magic Marker, and she boxes off and X's out every *NO* in every No Trespassing sign.

Example #3:

One day, they meet me at the umbrella stand for hot dogs for lunch. They'd taken a morning walk into a swamp behind the dunes.

"We're lucky we made it out," Irene says.

Without incident, my father says.

"Not without incident," Irene says, "but without damage. No leftover side effects."

Or maybe you mean holdover? my father asks.

"No, leftover, I mean. Left over after an incident or after an accident."

Residual? I say.

"No, I think leftover's closer to it," Irene says. "That's a good English word." She picks up my father's sketchbook.

We tracked a couple of rats, my father says.

"Two, possibly three," Irene says. "If one had an odd tail."

Or leash, my father says. We thought it could have been something like that, an odd tail, broken. Or a leash, if the thing was tame, you know. Something like that.

"These three rats," Irene says, "came down the dune to the water, either drank or picked up some scrap, turned around pretty cleanly, like an about-face, and walked back up the dune and over into that thicker grass."

They wouldn't drink salt water, my father says.

"Well, for whatever!" Irene says. "They went to the water and back around into that grass. The tracks were clear."

We could follow, my father says, and the one with the odd tail or leash, hung behind.

"Maybe it was dragging something with a tail," Irene says, "we considered that. But its feet didn't show any special weight or anything. And it had the odd tail on the way to the beach anyhow, so unless it was dragging something the whole way, that wouldn't account for the marks."

My father opens his jacket like a tablecloth and we sit on the beach for lunch. He explains about the swamp, how it was boggy rather than watery; he shows me his shoes which carry the color of the swampmuck, reddish black. He lays out on his jacket an hibiscus blossom, wilted, and he tells me about the ring of hibiscus shrubs the rats ran into—it looked like they were running by this time—and disappeared there, as if they'd dived.

"Or managed to leap to clumps of dry grasses," Irene says, "and leaped on from one clump to another to avoid our tracking them."

Did you see the rats? I ask.

"We saw everything *but* the rats," Irene says.

She opens my father's sketchbook and turns to the back where they keep a section of daily maps, and on a blank page I. draws out the meandering path of the rats, an oval for the particular swamp, some hatched lines for the dune grasses. My father adds in the details: breakers on the beach, posts of the broken-down fence they crossed.

———————————

Rats swim, of course. They do dive. It's all plausible.

My father draws a line of rat tracks, the scrape-mark of the odd tail, for the record.

Stalin drew wolf tracks on store lists, my father says. He draws a couple of wolf heads suspended in the margin.

"Stalin. Stalin. Somebody should shoot these guys when they sign their first order," Irene says.

My father's hand reaches for Irene's hair. He lifts a strand, he draws it across his cheek, and closes his eyes.

"End things right there," I. says. "Pull that trigger and then turn it around, take yourself out."

Somehow they're around to Svetlana again—out of the loop of mayhem, maybe, but in the middle of it.

My father loosens his muddy swamp shoes and kicks them off. They're crusted, like things washed up, strewn in a field after a flood.

My father leans over, separates Irene's hair, and lets his head settle in her lap. He's under her hair, and he'll stay there. They'll both nap.

That's how I find them, and it isn't the first time, when I walk down the beach and come back. It's always a shock: my father buried in a woman's hair.

My father's wolves have too much sweetness in them. He's better at vegetation, its edges, its teeth. Look at his Devil's Walking Stick.

Devil's Walking Stick

Those are fangs for you.

Devil's Walking Stick grows more than a foot a year. Every twig is covered with uneven thorns, sharp as broken glass. It's an oddity my father found on Black Log Mountain and brought back to propagate. The branches are flimsy and often crack or fall over in winter; the least bit of ice will break them.

But the hand can't touch them.

The tree spreads through a shallow root system that sprouts more sticks. My father planted the thing on the boundary line in the backyard. He thought it might make a fence, like concertina wire.

Irene was against the plan and, months later, in mid-winter, she was happy to see the ice damage, the broken-off branches. She raked up the sticks and burned them, the first day of spring.

My father's mother joined the Mennonite church—she turned plain—when she was thirty-five years old and my father was ten. In those days, the turn was visible, to the dark tones and ankle-length hems of orthodox dress. She let her hair grow and braided it and rolled it into a bun at the base of her neck, capped with a gauze prayer cap. She had dark hair and darker eyes, a small round face like a girl's, even then.

What was on her mind? What did she say? I ask him.

I don't know. She didn't say. She seemed the same to me, he says.

My father is vegetal, he is mineral, as wholly as animal. He isn't wary.

Some things slip by him, they just slip by. Other times, he'll take a small thing, a scrap, a word, and roll it around, and this one thing will grow and expand and proliferate, until all small things are wiped out entirely. He doesn't know when to quit.

He listens to the Phillies on the radio, he listens to soccer and hockey. He likes the back and forth of the field of play. He can picture the meandering paths the players create, moving around, that's what he sees. He's rooted in fields, maybe that's a way to explain it.

Things come and go, he says. All people do is play the field. A field of error. I'm a spectator to a wandering, my father says.

He refuses to acknowledge the most familiar terms: offense and defense. Superpower, blue ribbon, #1.

There's nothing to any of that, he says. It's the waywardness of things you want to see. The running around. And running around's got nothing to do with combat or war. Nothing at all.

He insists on it, and if I make a sour face, or turn around to do dishes, he coughs to clear up his voice, to keep going.

War's got nothing to do with anything, except maybe crime and delusion. It's dementia, he says, when people think *theirs* is the only world that counts. They overlord, overtake somebody else— or somebody else's *field*—and that's evil, and that's crime, and that's war.

He gasps in some air, and I sit down with him.

Is anything else evil? I ask him. I'm game.

I can't think of anything else.

Greed?

Same thing. You want more than you need, you want somebody else's things. Evil. Criminal.

Wanting more than you need is evil?

That's the beginning of it, sure. It goes from there. You got what you need, why want more?

What if you're starving and you steal something?

You need it. They should give it go you.

Who?

We should.

Stealing isn't criminal?

Not if you need it. Need it to survive. Otherwise, sure, it's greed, it's evil.

What about Irene?

I. breaks all the rules. He looks off, out the window. He's wavering.

She's evil?

I don't know, he says. She's harmless.

So far.

So far, my father says.

You're making exceptions. Where does that lead?

Yeah, my father says, and he's smiling right at me, we're all exceptions, mistakes, all error. And that's why you have to be so ruthless with yourself.

I'm trying to be ruthless with *you*, Daddy, I say. So you're saying stealing isn't evil, buying isn't evil, if you need something to survive?

That's it.

What about your drawings? Who needs them?

Well, they're pointless. Nobody needs them, true. But nobody wants them either.

If you need it, it's OK. If it's pointless, it's OK. Is that it?

That's it. That makes sense. I'll give you my sketchbook. And don't sell it because nobody should want it and nobody should have it who isn't given it.

What about those biographies you read? You bought them.

I need them! I need to know about these guys.

My father's a one-man band of moral noise: he's assembled it all, contrariwise—contradictions, contraindications. He's not a man of his culture, not a man of his times.

I tell him he runs counterclockwise.

He says, Well, I run. The aim is dust to dust.

For a man who centers an ethical system on error, on the impure, he can run with a pretty pure idea: the only purpose, beyond survival, is purposelessness. His moral ground is *geologic*—exist, be present as long, as harmlessly as possible, and then disappear.

That's it, he says. Evaporate our soggy selves, and rejoin the chemistries of dust. Go up in smoke. Never go out in glory. Rot. Rejoin the host of particulates.

My father re-draws those drawings of life cycles, the schematics that wheel an organism, or a hailstone, down and around and up and around full circle.

We're out here, my father says, on a goddamn field of error that webs everything together, and not just your temperate species, he says—and he points at me, jabs his finger at my neck—not just your swimmy organisms, but the whole blown stuff of the universe.

My father says it's good: everything goes up in smoke: horrors, rock, scissors, paper, a tobacco aroma in clouds, around the globe, in the streams of cirrus and in pools, eddies, passion, the haloes on radar of local weathers. Smoke rises in plumes of volcanoes, particulates from field dust, chimneys, from the rings blown out of Havana cigars, flesh, scorched earth, floodplains. Smell the sweetnesses, bitters, the air in the air, Tiflis to Lancaster, Santero, Aguila, Chuchin, there's a boundarylessness, body to body, after Stalin's death even Beria requested a smoke before he was shot, we know all about it, it's in our hair.

Before they joined the church and turned plain, Mennonite women did a lot of running around. That's what they called it, my father says. *Running around.*

They'd go off to the shore for a week in the summer; wearing fancy hats, they'd drive to Mount Gretna to pick huckleberries. On a Saturday afternoon, five or six of my grandmother's friends would take the bus to Lancaster, hang around at the Central Market.

Anything they did must have felt like running around. They were on their own, they could dance, wear lace, drink hard cider or elderberry wine in the tobacco stripping room, check out the open cars and the back roads. They turned plain when they wanted to, after they'd seen Atlantic City, or gone to Gettysburg a couple of times, after they married and had children.

Nobody said, now's the time, my father says. Nobody forced you or threatened hellfire. Nobody cut your throat.

It was like shedding a skin, unlayering. You gave away rings and your fingers lightened, lengthened. You gave away coats with polished buttons. You gave away the hats, feathered and pearled.

And after they joined the church, they still ran around. Chincoteague. The camp meeting grounds. Niagara Falls. Before and after, the same eyes are in the same face in my grandmother's photographs. The same crossed arms, easy around her waist.

But her hair is pulled back and her long neck shines. She's streamlined.

My father says he hardly noticed the change, and no wonder, look at her, then and then, that's Mae. She's the same woman running around.

Maybe lighter on her feet, my father says. More aerodynamic.

Svetlana claimed her father lived in an animal world—what did she mean? Guns and cigars? Skin, blood, bone, soft tissue?

Predator in his own species, was there a word in his mother tongue, on the tip of his mother's tongue, for him?

Stalin's mother Keke dressed like a nun in the last years of her life. She lived in a shack on the grounds of a Georgian palace; she refused to enter the main buildings.

He'd have done better, his mother is said to have said, to have become a priest.

Stalin never had blood on his hands. He made sure of that. He wore gloves. He made arrangements. He took some time in the country.

Animals that kill, the predators in the systems of nature, have blood at the corners of their mouths, blood between claws, under nails, blood in clots near the hair around their eyes, or blood on their bellies from where they have held something down and torn it apart.

They lick the blood off. Blood is food, as much as the meat of the flesh is food.

There is no name in nature for a predator who doesn't kill with its own body. Who won't lick the blood of the kill.

Who can't bloody himself and drink blood.

———————————

If not for nightmares, who'd know what to think?

I'd think about weather, roofs, food day to day, my father's hair. Friends, family, words that are talk like talk to the cat.

But nightmare spells it all out. You can't miss the lettering in blood, fire, steam, piss. The hydraulic machinery coming at you, buckling the landscape and filling silos with sand. Stalin catapulted into the yard. A brutal body, in dark gray wool.

Out the kitchen window, Stalin stands in the backyard, talking with my father.

The first time my father appears in a dream, he is outside with Stalin, not me.

My father is wearing a long wool coat and a Russian fur hat, with earflaps.

Words huff out of their mouths and take visible shape, like the words in balloons in the comics. It is not idle talk.

It's skywriting, smoke from cigars.

I listen hard and I squint my eyes to read, but I can't hear the words and I can't read them.

All or nothing, my little Housekeeper, Stalin wrote Svetlana.

Stalin rebuilt each of his houses. It was a cycle—things held for a while and then they turned.

Stalin couldn't accept the wear and tear, the dacha at Pervukhino, Kuntsevo, and he couldn't stand being snookered, as Svetlana learned to call it, by the easy-going plumbers and carpenters with their kits and lunch sacks from any village in the vicinity.

Before a door warped, before a house turned against him, he had it wrecked or reworked into a new arrangement of rooms with a green-painted door that opened easily, the latchplate good brass. Stalin opened the door for Svetlana, let her run in. He held the door wide, to breathe in the scoured air, with the cut of new plaster in it. The inside air of the inside rooms gathered around him at the door. It was better than air by the Black Sea.

Papa, come in! Svetlana called.

I'm breathing, Stalin said. He stood there a few minutes.

A few minutes, every few years.

Irene has converted my father to her religion of trespass. He is planning to go away, someplace where he has no right to be.

Someplace where he can turn plainer and more plain.

He promises me he won't die until he gets back. But meantime, while he can, he will go somewhere else—another continent, another culture. He'll wander off into a desert. For no reason. No purpose.

An American outlaw, not out for success, he says. Not out for the tour or the dollars. Up to no good—that's good.

He coughs, and the cough shakes him hard. He bends his knees and steps backwards.

Is that good? he says, when he looks around at me. Is that possible?

My father thinks Irene Iruskaiya might shoot him because she knows he wants to be dead.

He pulls me by the wrist to two kitchen chairs in the middle of the back yard. Don't worry, he says. When I get back, we'll beat her to it.

These two chairs are plank-seated schoolhouse chairs and when we sit down on them, the legs push into mud. The frost is just out of the ground, though not the chill, and a couple strands of cold move around my ankles.

I'll tell you exactly what to do, he says.

On a tractor, my father still looks healthy enough—the pretzel roll to his arms when he turns the steering wheel; the pump through his knees, braking. But on a chair in the yard, look, he is ghost daddy—spun-out hair, long bones. His knees bend at a bad angle under his trousers, and his hands, holding mine, could be cut-outs, the knuckles oversize clasps, hooked bone to bone under waxed paper.

Nothing flashy, he says. Nothing splashy.

My father tells me a person should not take longer to die than to be born.

You slipped in, my father says. Your mother didn't blink.

That's not how it was with Jamella.

She was crossways, but even so, you had her pretty fast. It wasn't more than a day, was it? Nature is economical, my father says. I think we should try to match it.

A gun is fast, I say.

A gun is a waste, my father says. It's loud, it's a mess, it scares people.

Does it scare you?

Irene with a gun scares me, he says. She wants drama. She wants a dramatic scene. But you and me, he leans over, tilts the chair, we'll make it invisible. One of the great invisibilities.

He taps his fingertips on his thigh, and then I hear he is counting. Five. Six! *Invisibilities* has six *i*'s, he says. Think about that. The *i*'s have it! Know any other words with six *i*'s?

His hair blows around, a strand into his mouth. He taps his foot. If all these goddamn *I*'s would let themselves disappear, he says, just a couple of trails on the planet, hell, we'd all die happy.

Will you die happy, Daddy?

Oh, no doubt about it, sweet pie. No doubt about that at all.

3

Something Is Going to Rip Him Apart

That's how it was that the spring before he died, my father lived at the edge of a desert, in a dirt-floored hut, where he had no reason to be.

It was a shack, with no door, a roof that was two galvanized sheets, wired to posts. He taught reading, in a language he hadn't quite learned.

He told me he planted tobacco seeds, seeds fine as ground pepper—he planted a pinch—in dirt he sterilized on a campstove.

For the flowers, he said, but he wouldn't see the flowers.

For the velvet leaves, he said. Nobody will know it's tobacco.

————————————

He had no mailing address, although he sent me e-mail from the gas station at Knot.

Knot here! was his greeting. No mortification of the flesh.

But wasn't it?

Did he think that there—or anywhere—he could do good?

Be good? Do wrong? Do nothing?

He did plenty. He hauled water from a well. He brushed a dirt yard with a weedstraw broom. He walked to a concrete block school and he walked back. He drew sticks and foliage he couldn't name. He drew wolf ears among leaves.

I should teach *nonsense*, he wrote me. Maybe I am. They read me stories I can't understand. They read one book after another. Do you think it's nonsense?

As for himself, he stopped reading. Here, he said, before he left, I'm not taking books. I leave Stalin for you.

The night my father flies out of the country, Stalin takes the roof off the front porch of my house and leans it against the chimney. He hauls in a bulldozer and levels the yard, and he plants rows of chiseled columns, huge as smokestacks, like the ones in the

Hall of Columns where the Burial Commission laid him in state. Stalin has nothing against me, I know it, but he throws me, like sod, against the brick wall of the house. Both of my legs are broken, sticks in pieces. And then Stalin brings down the wall with his mechanized arms that can bring down anything.

Jamella, my daughter, is back from a dig. She's been away two years, and now she's taken some weeks to meet Irene—"I've got to see the hair," she says—and to see her grandfather when he comes home.

"Don't expect me to stay until he's dead," she says.

Jamella has black hair that shines almost purple, iridescent, and she crops it close, high over her ears. Her ears are her grandfather's ears, large and angled out, like ears cupped out by hands, for better hearing.

She brought a machete back as a present for me. She's got a plan to hack a path through the underbrush along the creek. For years, the creek has been out of reach, gone in the tangle of briars, nettles and heaps of fallen branches.

Years ago, we farmed right to the stream and there's evidence for it: where the stream comes close to the edge of the woods is a dump of fieldstones, a half-dam, hauled there on sledges drawn by horses.

When we quit farming tobacco and let that field go, the locusts sprouted first, dense as shrubbery, then wild grape that bent over branches, and under that everything sprouted, a rot-gut local jungle: five-foot stinging nettles, greenbrier, raspberry, poison ivy, cleaver, stick-tight. A half-mile stretch along the stream disappeared. Ordinary brush and scrub tangled, twisted up from the sand banks, draped from cottonwoods, and threw vines over in layers of leaf and stalk stuffing that could have been bedding on dead branches.

It's a mess.

"I've never seen the place," Irene says.

"It's so pretty," Jamella says. "I saw it, as a kid. I'd sneak back there and crawl under vines to the creek."

There are two sycamores we can see from the house, towering, spared by somebody, maybe my father, who has drawn the bleached bark in his sketchbook.

I'd like to see the water again.

Jamella says, "We could hack a trail with the machete, keep it low, cut it just enough to twist through."

"The more hidden the better," Irene says. "Get there like any muskrat could. Polecat could."

Jamella and Irene are helping me pick plums for a tart, for the welcome-back party next week. We've spread a bedsheet under the plum tree in the backyard, and I'm on the second branch, shaking it with my feet. Jamella takes the machete and whacks another branch with the flat of the blade. These are greengage plums, some not much bigger than somebody's thumb, and they rattle onto the ground like pits more than fruit falling. Irene scoops them up in her scarf—she's got the scarf looped around her neck at one end, and the other end's opened up like an apron she can fill and haul into the house, one-handed.

"Do you think Svetlana picked plums for her daddy?" Irene

says. "Do you think she cooked anything? He wouldn't have trusted even her, would he?, to keep poison out of the kettle."

"There's a poison plum near our dig," Jamella says. "We were warned off the first day by the mayor. They're such an unusual peach sort of plum he knew somebody'd try it."

"Come on!" Irene says. "Sometimes I think *everything's* edible and all these fear tactics are a scheme, you know—to keep plums for the mayor!"

What about poison ivy? I say.

"I've never got it," Irene says. "I've picked it, too. I stuck the berries in a vase for your daddy. It didn't bother me at all."

"Well, *these* plums are okay," Jamella says. "We've eaten them for years."

"I know. The plum tart. I bet you could cook up a plum tart for that mayor, too, and everybody'd feast just fine."

"I'm not gonna try it," Jamella says. With a wild swing of the machete, she chips some bark off a branch. "This thing needs sharpening," she says.

I'd keep an eye on Irene, wherever she was. She'd pick, on purpose, a handful of poison berries and throw them into a stew for Stalin. She'd get caught, and killed, of course. She'd expect that.

I watch her twist the scarf full of plums until they're twirled tight in the sack of it. She tosses the sack over her shoulder—a hump on her back now—and she walks to the porch. On the back step, she detours around Jamella, who's got the machete propped on one knee. With a file in her hands, Jamella swings her arms back and forth like somebody rocking a babe, sharpening the blade.

Svetlana never poisoned her father; it never crossed her mind. She never poisoned anybody. He never asked, of course; he never ordered. Would she have obeyed?

In one photograph, Stalin scoops her up at the door to the apartment, like a husband with a bride. All of this scooping up and carrying around, why do men do it except that they can? Stalin can do whatever he wants. He can carry Svetlana to the door or swing her up into his face for a kiss. He can set her down so suddenly she slips and her hand scrapes in the gravel. He can carry a woman to a cot, a corpse to a ditch, a girl to a branch of a tree. Svetlana is almost full grown, an armful of girl in her wide schoolgirl shoes, her checked blouse and her striped skirt.

She's got a rump on her, Beria said, behind his hand to the photographer, who lived long enough to report this.

Irene decided to fly over to meet my father, spend a few days with him, and then fly him back.

Jamella said, "Why don't you go, Mother?"

I told her it was Irene's hands he could hold now. We've got stuff to pick, I said. Yard to mow.

"Yeah, that's critical," Jamella said.

Well, can't you picture them wandering around in the desert, checking the vegetation, talking to all the students?

"I can picture it. I see it," Jamella said. "I can see you wandering around, too."

It was months later I heard the story from Irene how, the last day they spent in the village, my father rescued a dog in a flood.

A flood in the desert? I asked her.

"A flash flood. It was the edge of a desert," she said.

There was no rain there, just the flood. I. said that my father figured things out at a glance: the rate of flow of the water through the gully, his own walking speed and angle in that current to the dog ripping by.

My father strode into the twisting water, up to his chest pocket. He snagged the dog by the neckhairs, swung around, and walked back to shore taking each step slow, with a wash of foam kicking up in his armpits, bobbing the dog around.

At the edge of the gully, my father climbed a mud bank onto a wide slab of rock and set the dog down. The dog shook itself twice and leaped off through the brush before anybody could say *good dog*, or pet it, or get a leash on it.

My father stripped to his underwear, and Irene brought him a beach towel that he wrapped around his waist, a flashy sarong.

Wasn't he breathing hard? I asked.

"*I* was!" Irene said.

My father got some congratulations from a couple of kids there, though it was not especially risky, Irene didn't think, what he'd done.

"And nothing, of course," Irene said, "not even the dog, to show for it."

———————————

Scraps, bits, dust, nothing. I might as well be Jamella at an ancient site. Brushing bones, shards. The scraps say something, but who can sketch in what's missing? Irene never writes a word—she X's them out. My father draws wolf ears and leaves.

It's easy for Jamella. She says, "That's what there is. There are bits and pieces. That's what there is, and that's what's left."

She never brings anything back, not bone, not bracelet. "You put everything back as it was, you have to," she says, "and re-bury it."

Stalin's funeral, anybody there could tell you, was no simple matter, not with the gaping hole in procedure and protocol, with Stalin himself out of the picture.

The Burial Commission chose the Hall of Columns for Stalin's lying-in-state. They assembled heaps of ferns, real and artificial flowers—all the flowers in Moscow—in appropriate funereal sprays, brass planters and vases next to the coffin and its cloak of pleated satin.

The Burial Commission insisted on the longest-term embalmment. None of that dust to dust.

Stalin was drained, gutted, de-muscled, sterilized, and pumped with a putty. Taxidermists worked on the nose, lips, ears, the eye-lashes, hair.

Still, Stalin's sleep among flowers was not restful. People kept their eyes open. They watched his lips, watched his earlobe, the large one facing the line of mourners. The ear didn't move.

In the Hall of Columns, the mourners didn't speak. But outside, they shouted at each other and pushed one another aside. Long lines of ambulances carried away mourners, stampeded, suffocated, crushed. Hundreds died.

Svetlana saw nothing. At the right moment, she stepped up to the coffin, she kissed the forehead of Stalin, and then they shut the lid with the window in it. Stalin's face appeared under glass.

In the mausoleum, anybody could look at Stalin's face. He was right there. Until a Re-Burial Commission was appointed, years later, with orders to put him underground, Stalin stayed put.

Spring in the desert did my father good. For three months, he walked, his lungs worked and his voice rested. In the hut, he breathed dry air, the flavor of sorghum in his throat; he said he slept all night.

Coming home was the first step of a fare-thee-well. I look at my father and I can see it, veins under the skin, translucent. He's lost muscle.

I say to myself, that's him, that's my father, who won't last long.

Back here, the mists and weighted humidities, blue in the distance and green or gray in the hollows, slow him down.

He needs oxygen, and we get a cart, some tanks, the tubes. He says it is not in keeping with nature's scheme to carry around his own air, and he argues with me for days about it; but he must know he needs more time—to convince me to help him. To con Irene, forestall her own plots to help him out.

Every night at dinner, Irene offers, "Anytime you say. You can count on me."

She keeps the gun loaded. She swears she won't lose her nerve.

I. is lucky at games of chance. She says she always has been. At the grocery store raffle, a couple days after the plum tart party, Irene wins a trip to the Mall of America, a $500 spending spree, and she takes it. She swears she'll buy whatever she brings back, and it won't be anything useful, just junk, just something to spread out on the table and look at and try to guess where it came from.

And why, my father says.

And how, I say.

When my father walked in the door and saw Jamella, his voice cranked up a notch or two, he straightened his back, and he called, Jammie! Sweetie! and opened his arms. She ran right to him, and if he could have, he would have scooped her up.

Since she was born, they have hugged each other, kissed each other hello and good-by. Jamella still holds his hand when they go for a walk. He leans over when he talks to her, and their breathing mixes, a fog between them.

My theory is: affection, like baldness, skips a generation.

But then, how could Svetlana leap in her father's arms? How could Stalin reach for her and lift her?

With me, my father will talk, he'll dispute. He wants me to know what he thinks. I want to know. I grill him, interrogator. So what if we sold the frontage? I say. Once you buy something, isn't it already split up? Name me one thing that's absolutely whole.

We take it all back to first principles.

If dialogue is an embrace, we are loving and mightily loved. I quiz him, I quarrel, I take him to task.

Sometimes I think, I'm a wall, a sounding board. When my father talks to me, he hears what he has to say. He thinks things through and I love that turn, when he changes his mind, or I change mine.

We are so close in this, why should we go arm in arm to say fare-thee-well?

———————

If you can't ask your father, Is that good?, and can't say, No, it's not, what's an embrace but another measure of things not said? Another power play, like arm wrestling.

Svetlana arm-wrestled Stalin, he encouraged it. She had the forearm, the rump, the leverage. She took to public ceremony. She kissed the forehead of Stalin even when he was dead and unmuscled, and had nothing to say to her or to anybody. No say at all.

———————

After breakfast my father carries his cup of coffee to the bench on the deck and I push his cart beside him. He's got his binoculars around his neck and the weight pulls his head forward.

He says, If I'm going to die in a field, I might as well know the field.

That's the first I hear about his plans.

If something's going to rip me apart, he says, and it's clear this is already a fact in his mind, I want— and he points over the woods, and there they are— those four vultures. And a couple of coyotes.

Jamella is sleeping late. She's generous with herself, and with everybody else. If she's mad, it's never the person—"it's the issue," she says. She believes this.

Well, you can be sweet, you're never here, I tell her. You're nomadic, I say, and look at her, she looks it, even in a house: snipped hair, bony wrists and knuckles knobbed and shiny—not like brass knuckles, not like mine—but like hammered brassy jewelry.

Jamella has been on every continent that's not ice; she buys the local shoes and uses them—wooden shoes, straw shoes, most of them ordinary leather strap shoes. She comes back here every couple of years and she'll rest for a few months, sleep until mid-afternoon, walk with her grandfather, visit Louella and Dominic at the restaurant and cook with them on weekends.

She always knows the time of day, whenever she wakes up, she just knows it. And she has a sense of season, too, like somebody taking a flock of goats up and down mountain passes, or those women in brown capes known for crossing the Gobi Desert, the first traders.

Last night, my father sat across the table with Jamella, patting her hand, a slow pat pat, and we checked out the aerial map. There was no creek. You could pick out the hay field with its yellowing cut lines, the green old growth woods, and then there was this darkest *thatchery*, Jamella called it.

The water's there, my father said. With a purple marker, he sketched in a line for the creek and twisted it through some U-turns he could remember. He X'd a spot where we'd step out of the timothy field, closest to the water, and start cutting the trail. Jamella, who's used to expeditions and is, even at home, gung-ho, said we should take a daypack—water, bug spray.

The tree book, my father said. Who knows what's back there.

———————

This morning my father sent me to town to buy hedge clippers, the expensive kind with the coil shock. You can clip, he said.

He dug leather gloves out of the cardboard box in the closet. You take them, he said. I'm not allergic.

I'm not allergic either.

And you're not terminal, my father said. Mortal. But not terminal. Take the gloves.

———————

My father's doing what he should not be doing—hacking at

poison ivy with a machete, one-handed, and with the other hand, dragging the two-wheeled aluminum cart and a tank of oxygen. The breathing tubes are taped to his nose, a see-through Dali mustache, and he's sweating, but not as much as you'd expect, a bit on his forehead, a few drops that haven't dropped yet.

In the back yard, where the grass meets the weed field, he slashes at burdock and Queen Anne's lace. A few steps into the weeds, he practices on stalky brush, the autumn olives and red-twig dogwood. Sticks fly and fall, leaves flip on the ground, belly up.

He's getting himself in shape.

He wheels the oxygen cart around, and one-handed with the machete, lops off exactly one flowerhead from the goldenrod, or— when it comes to the paw paws and little maples—he props the cart against his thigh and swings with both hands, hacks the stalks through, and lays them down, clean.

He's something to see, you'd never predict it in a back yard: an old man whirling like that with a weapon and a cart, his long hair fanned out, blurred metallic at his neck.

The blade whirrs, almost hums when he circles. He helicopters.

These are not approved moves, I don't think. I don't approve them.

———————————

Awake, Jamella argues that the machete is dull now and a danger to use. She offers to sharpen it. She knows how, it's one of her jobs.

My father says, The sharper the better.

It sounds to me like one of those phony formulas: sharp equals safe; ignorance equals bliss; healthy equals happy.

I make a pot of coffee while Jamella sits on the bench out back. With the machete handle propped against her belly, she takes a file and she leans and presses and sharpens the blade. How many edges are there to sharpen? One? Two? Buckle my shoe?

From here, with her back to me, it looks like she's working out. She rocks and leans towards her toes, her clogs.

Take your time, Jammie, my father says, and he goes outside with her.

I feel like saying, Time is money.

But that's stupid and a lie, I don't believe it. I stick my face in the coffee mug and suck up some steam. I look down there at my forehead floating, a moonscape, and I listen. Someplace else, some other territory off the maps, time would be what? A meander? Maybe it would come and go, stay a while, take off.

Not here. I count a pulse pushing through my neck at exactly the rate of Jamella's stretches.

There is a moment when she stands at the door, blood falling fast from her hand to her jeans, that I think it's my father's blood Jamella has somehow caught and carried in.

"This has never happened," she says.

I grab some dishtowels from a drawer and start wrapping her hand.

"I caught my thumb. I can't believe it."

Where's your grandfather? I ask.

Jamella turns to the door, and there he is, pulling at the

cart—one wheel's bumped the door jamb. He's breathing so hard he's rocking himself up and down.

How bad is it? he says.

"It's still bleeding," Jamella says. "It's deep, but it doesn't hurt a bit. This has not ever happened. Ever."

The bleeding soaks through the towels, and Jamella looks away at her other hand, the other thumb. Air rasps through her throat.

You're not going to die, I tell her.

Well, she is, my father says. He's got the oxygen tank through the door, and he takes Jamella's good hand and holds it against his chest.

But not yet, he adds. Not now.

Jamella laughs with him, just her front teeth showing.

You'll need stitches, I say.

I've got a long kitchen towel tied around her hand, and the bleeding slows.

Jamella sits down and sets her wrapped hand in her lap. She watches my father pull paper towels from the roll and wipe blood off the floor.

Soon she is calm, ready to walk to the car. "No problem," she says.

I don't remember going outside, but I'm holding the car door open, and Jamella climbs in the back seat with my father, who's already loaded his gear there and is waiting for her.

At the hospital, we take our time. An hour. An hour and a half. That's not much, out of a day.

The emergency room isn't busy, and my father talks about managed care with Albert who's on duty at the desk, and time passes. I take Jamella a cup of coffee from the machine while she's being stitched up. The doctor says nothing until he's tied the last thread. "That'll do you," he says then.

We're back at the house by lunch.

My father is restless. He takes a bag of nuts from the refrigerator and passes them around.

Jamella kicks off her shoes and sprawls in a chair at the window, her hand propped on the windowsill. The thumb's huge, wrapped in gauze, immobilized with a metal splint like a cage around it.

You know, we could still hack the path, my father says.

Jamella sits up. One-handed, she pulls on her black rubber pig boots. She won't be any help with the work, but she wants to come along anyway. She says she can carry the backpack with water for us.

Sure, I say. The more risk the better.

"Don't be sour," Jamella says. "I'll just sit."

With all the equipment to lug along, we decide to drive out the lane and park at the edge of the field. I've got the clippers, the leather gloves, and my father carries the machete.

"I was almost finished," Jamella says. "That'll cut fine for you."

Put the weaponry in the trunk, I say.

"It is not weaponry, Mother," Jamella says. "Those are *tools*."

All right. She does not understand my vocabulary, I am not sour. I am bitter. Bitter is fine, it makes sense. Bitter is seeing clear. I am happy, I mean by this. And calm.

Look at the way we eat cashews at the car and skip lunch.

When everything but the oxygen tank is in the trunk, Jamella and my father climb in the back seat again, careful with the tank, careful with the thumb, and we head out the lane.

Well, I'm a goddamn chauffeur, I tell them.

"Of the not-dead?" Jamella says.

This crisis with the machete has lifted her spirits.

They're laughing back there, and that's fine with me. I speed up at an old plow line, a real bump in the road, and for the hell of it, give everybody a good jolt.

My father and I walk from the car through some timothy, to the edge of the woods. There we stop. You know how it is. When you cross that line, from a wide-open field into a woods, you gasp, sunlight switches to off, it's a shock, and you slow down.

The first step in, you inhale, and you feel air you don't usually feel move over your tongue and into the cave of the back of the throat. You have to wait until your eyes adjust to the dark and then to the mottled light, patched and floating around.

In the minutes my father and I stand there, our breathing

slows and pretty soon it matches the sound of the woods' iron-lung respiration, those noises like variable-speed fans and streamers somewhere.

It's cool and humid. Another climate. My shoulders are damp, like armpits, and the whole place is inside-out, gone under and into a territory all interior. Even the ground feels fleshed, cushy with leaf-rot and the sponge of root fibers, webs, and wood digested to gel.

Two steps in, it's impossible to walk, the tangle of briar is so thick. My father takes a few cuts with the machete, and then he can move. What's probably a deer trail opens up enough for a human being. He goes ahead, rough-cutting in front of him and taking a few swipes overhead, although he's bent over so much that the path behind, where I am, is a crouching path.

The oxygen cart makes a wheel-track, and that's my guide, the two lines I clip between.

I trim down the briars and the nettles low to the trail, snip them down until I can see one boot, and then I step ahead, stooped, and clip down to that boot. Shrapnel of twig, leaf meal, bark debris flies back at me, overhead. My father's having a good time. And I think, too, this isn't work. It's what somebody familiar with mammoths, say, would do to get to the water. Swing a weapon, step shod or unshod on leaves, and hack out a path. The more hidden the better.

I can see the slashed greenery, but I can't see my father. I'm hung up in a wild grape vine that's coiled through some raspberry stalks twisted around one leg, and a heap of those pale green cleavers, flimsy stalks that stick like Velcro, hang off my shoulder and down my back. I don't know where Jamella is. She said she'd sit in the car and maybe nap.

After a while, my father calls, I'm at the creek!

I'll be there! I yell back. Hang on!

By the time I'm untangled and at the creek, he's gone off downstream. The path opens at the water along a straightaway, and it's a rippled-up creek, full of rocks and snags. The creek is a clearing, and light splays out from it, iridescent on leaves—they look oily, mother-of-pearlish. The overhead green cools down, it lightens up, and there's a sparkle on things because of the damp. Spiderwebs show up, and they're in the nettles like nests, and tightroped across the water.

My father has foot-stomped this trail—it's more open here at the creek bank and he wouldn't need the machete.

In a minute, I spot him leaning against a tree, uprooted from the bank and fallen over the water. He's at the root-end, which is a stub now, the dirt and roots long rotted off, although there's still the stump like a high-backed chair behind him. The trunk of the tree has settled into the water, sunk below the surface, and when I get close to it, I can see the water, silvery, pouring over it—it looks like stainless steel, molten and flowing—one long breaker the width of the creek.

Pretty enough for you? my father says.

Not bad, I say.

We sit there a while just looking around until Jamella comes along with the backpack.

"This isn't what I remember as a kid," she says.

She ooohs and ahhhs. And why not? It's not often you go to a place you haven't seen in twenty years, and it's better-looking than it was in the past.

Jamella says, "Yeah. This is wild."

I walk back a bit, to re-clip the path on the stream bank, really get it low so you don't have to watch your feet there but can walk along looking at the water. The creek is full of round stones, some rust-colored, some almost bluish. The bank is sandy, with a little drop-off, and across the other side is a much steeper cliff bank, with dirt slides where deer come down. I see some raccoon tracks on a sand bar, and a couple of clamshells they've cleaned out.

The place is crammed, I feel dizzy like I do at a mall, with too much to see, and I finally just sit on a rock and try to see what's what. I don't know the names of half the plants—I think the stalky weed, all the white flowers, leaning out over the water is water hemlock. Or cow parsnip. There's bergamot, and greenbrier with seed pods like golfballs. We'll get out the books tonight and make a list: turtlehead, silkweed, boneset. And cardinal flower, the blood-red one, I pick it to show Jamella.

I'm going to hold the stalk against her hand and say, I recognize this.

When I turn back to call her, well, look at them, there they are. They're slumped together. My father is half keeled over. His shirt has a vine on it, some splotchy stains. Jamella has sunk her whole face in my father's hair. The man looks done for.

But no, he's fine, he's just bent at the waist. He is kissing the metal splint on her thumb.

I stand still and listen. If Jamella is talking, it sounds like leaves. I know I've known them all my life, but when she drops in, and he walks out, it's a different place, and they're newcomers, forest people from who knows where. Not this neck of the woods.

———————————

"Well!" Irene says, when she returns.

You'd think she'd be pissed, that she missed out on the footpath action, but no. She hugs Jamella. She kisses my father's lips. "Look here!"

And out of a shopping bag of souvenirs, along with some scarves and a fancy spring-form tart pan, she pulls several large orange signs: Trespassers Welcome.

"What luck!" she says. "We can put them around the boundary. See who finds the place."

———————————

When I'm dead, you can let her shoot me, my father says.

———————————

He gives me the box of tobacco leaves. I think it is my inheritance. Seven leaves. Jamella and I lay them out on the table. They are older than she is.

Still damp in damp weather; dry in dry.

Jamella takes off her Caribbean shoe and sets it beside a leaf—the color's the same, gold gone to leather. I count one, two, three, and, we've done it before, we shut our eyes, lean into the leaves, breathe—and there's the dirt field.

Clay. Tobacco juice. Dust.

"Recipe for pie," Jamella says.

Recipe for me.

———————————

What was Svetlana made of?

Books? Paper?

Whatever she held in her hands.

The violin. The pen.

Whatever gave her a thrill.

Fashion. Duty. The liberal arts.

After what her mother did, she said, she could never hold a gun or fire one. A good student, such a girl.

No farming, no politics, either. "So dirty," she said.

"Live and let live," she told Irene.

Who told my father.

Who, shaking his head, told me.

That's fine, he says, if you're living. If you're dying, it's another story. There's no letting live. No going on, no ongoing. No next time, no plot. Except the plot you pick out, the place you sit down, set yourself up to lie down.

My father talks and talks. It's not easy for him. He keeps adjusting the oxygen, sucking it down. His head snaps back when he inhales and sometimes he shuts his eyes for so long it gives me a scare.

But then he blinks them open, lifts both legs up and props them on the porch rail, and he looks like a man with plenty of time for lounging around.

A bed's not a good plot, he says. You know what I'm talking about?

I know.

What you have to do is not sound an alarm, he says, that's

all I'm asking. I've got a good plot, there's a backrest, I'll be fine.

But how do you know how long it will take? What if you time this all wrong and end up sitting out there in the rain for a couple of days.

Doesn't matter. I've got a cover letter for you. It's written. I'll just date it when I leave. 'Gone camping. Be back in three days.'

But Jamella's still here, I say. She'd be out there after you, you know it.

No, I'll work this out with her, my father says. She'll take off, she's seen enough.

And he coughs hard, and then goes into a fit of coughing that rattles him so much his legs slip off the railing.

Jamella opens the back door and stands there. She's making up her mind, he's right. And she says so.

"I'm booking a flight. How does that sound?"

That's good, my father says, his voice a whisper, coughed out. You don't have to come back, you know. Wait til I'm burnt bones, you can dust your arms.

Jamella sinks on her knees beside him. She falls all apart. She puts her arms around his shoulders, she's holding him down in the chair and crying on his head. "I will, I'll do that," she says.

Then she stands up, swings around to another chair on the porch and sprawls. "I've got your bones anyhow!" she says. And she pounds on her knees and then kicks out a foot to touch his leg.

It's the truth, my father says. You've got my bones. Where's Irene? She's got my voice. And you, he turns to me, you've got the blood and guts.

You said it, I say.

Flesh and blood, that's you, my father says. Flesh made word.

It's *word made flesh*, I say.

Not in my book, my father says.

If he were all words, of course, he wouldn't die. He does *look* like a book—he's folding forward more every day. His arms pull in and the skin smooths out like paper, or papyrus, with bluish lines, and his backbone's a book spine, and the book practically shut.

But his words are air, in and out, and they're still taking shape. Out of his mouth. Off the page. His words are carbon dioxide—food for leaves.

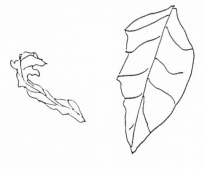

I help him pack his camping gear: blankets, a Thermos for water, a shoebox with pens and paper. It all fits in a leather backpack that will be his pillow.

Think of it this way, he says. I'm stalking predators. I'll find them because they'll find me.

He is thinking of Stalin, his eye for prey, his pack of violences. My father, propped on the blanket beside the rock, his body the bait, watches Stalin come out of the woods. Or, Stalin swoops down in a whirlwind, his arms caped, his feet set for landing, and then he hits, with his grid-work boot soles hard on the ground next to my father's hand. Stalin shakes off his stealth garments of wind and cloud. He shimmers there, dry-cleaned, his jacket buckled, and the buckle shined. If he pulled his pistol and shot my father, my father would claim that Stalin surrendered. If Stalin cut off my father's leg and ate a thick slice of it like a chop, my father would celebrate armistice. In this subversion of victory, my father feeds death to Stalin, offers him all the prey he can handle, a head on a platter, more flesh than Stalin could cart to the woods, more blood than he could drink or drain into his canteen to carry back with him into the whirlwind.

Whole suns collapse on themselves and suck space with them into a hole. The universe makes sense.

Jamella is back at work digging bones. She e-mails me that the site has been looted—somebody's walking around somewhere trying to sell a gold buckle and the skull of a boy.

She asks, "Is he still breathing?"

She knows the answer is yes, because she will hear about it as soon as the answer is no.

But I understand why she wants to picture my father

opening and closing his mouth, the oxygen tank turned to *off*, set aside. He flares his nostrils. He leans back.

At her computer, Jamella leans back, too. She breathes in, and breathing out, her breath latches onto some of the current that's headed across the Gulf, aimed fast up the Mississippi for that sharp turn along the Ohio, and the jet stream pulls a branching of clouds overhill at Wheeling and overland from there, across the Appalachians through the Cumberland Gap to the Susquehanna, its rivery mists slung low, stalled here.

He takes in a breath. He's still breathing.

———————————————

Irene has a dinner planned at her house. But my father cannot get out of bed. He lies there with his eyes closed and doesn't say yes and doesn't say no.

She says on the phone, "I'm afraid we waited too long. He can't shoot himself in bed."

He's not going to shoot himself anywhere, I say.

"Well, you know. You know what I mean."

Why don't you bring dinner here? I've got some wine.

"A last supper?" she says. "Or next-to-last, who can tell."

.He doesn't look good, I tell her. I can't get him to say anything, but I think he hears.

"He'll hear us," she says.

———————————————

She's gone all out. Watercress salad. Squash blossom soup pureed for my father. Bread she has baked, Russian rye. We set the card table by my father's bed, bring in the wine bottle, and eat there and drink there and watch my father's face.

When I. talks about her own exit—how she'll sell her house and move to some other climate when my father's gone—he doesn't open his eyes.

"He's nodding his head, I think," she says.

His mouth opens and I hear something. We both listen. His lips shut, and his jaw slips to one side, as if his tongue's scanning there or counting his teeth, his gold crowns.

Irene holds my father's hand and his fingers tap now and then in her palm. I watch his face and I watch his fingers. He's still full of motion, if you catch the lips at the right moment, or the hand.

———————————

Irene says she talked to a guy named Timothy in a Stalin chat room, and he claimed to have seen Svetlana walking along with a three-footed cane, on the streets of a suburb of London.

You go into chat rooms?

"I go wherever I want," she says. "Since your father hasn't been walking so much, I've been on the computer a lot. This guy lives near the rest home she's in, and he says she walks very slow, unsteady. She never looks both ways at intersections, she just sets the cane in the gutter and steps off the curb. He's afraid she'll get hit one of these days."

Svetlana an old woman at last. "Where does she think she's going?" I. says.

In the morning, my father is fine. He's sitting on the edge of the bed, his feet under the card table. I take his pulse and it's flimsy, too quiet.

Can you get up? I ask him.

He holds out his arm, but then he gasps, and slumps back against the pillow, he's lopsided there, one arm behind his head, the other arm fallen to the side. He's embarrassed with the dramatics of his body, and he shuts his eyes.

But I can see through him. He's afraid he won't get out of bed; he's afraid he's waited too long and missed his chance at a simple departure, walking out and sitting down.

I can see through his skin to the veins in his wrist. I can see tendons.

He takes measured breaths through his open mouth while I hook up the oxygen.

In a minute he whispers, Get me some paper. I want to write that note I said I would write.

My father has a fake tooth, an incisor, hooked with a gold clasp. It's on his nightstand, and I pick it up and hand it over. He snaps it in, and his gap-toothed smile disappears. He's ready for work. He sets his feet on the floor.

You could make a ring, he says. He taps his tooth.

What? I don't wear jewelry.

It's no jewel, it's a tooth. Porcelain, he says. It'd look good on you.

I have not asked my father:
How plain can a sentence be?
Jesus wept.
No.
Oh.
How plain can a body be?
A cell, a molecule.
A dot.
Oh.
Is the dot at the end of a sentence a body?

At dinner Irene told me she wishes my father would, if he could, tattoo his body all over, complicate his skin with line-drawings of leaves, tobacco and curlicue foliage all over before he dies.

I dream, I told her, but you're the dreamer.

This is it, my father says.

And as if I'm Jamella, a girl again, he takes my hand, I can't believe it, and he kisses my knuckles.

I can't say a thing, I just shake my head, which is *yes*. His hand is dry, cool in this heat, and I turn it over and bring his hand like the breathing mask to my mouth, and kiss the palm.

The sun is no more of a spotlight than usual, but it blasts with such force onto the grass that it smells like cut grass, aromatic, a mowed field, with the hay scent that borders on rot, all the cuts clean and flowing with stalk juice. I close my eyes and my father's hand smells like the yard and the yard smells like hay and hay like tobacco, leaf over leaf, cut and heaped all afternoon in the field. There's nothing else like it, things fed by fluid, drained and drying. It's the smell of thick stalk, and ink. And there, with the smell, the accompaniment of flies, the yard full of them, buzzing, brushes on cymbals, and the aimless takeoffs and flailings that somehow land them on any wound or orifice, the last damp in dry, the hole in the ground.

I open my eyes and there's a fly at the corner of my father's eye. He brushes it away. There's another one on the top of his head.

My father says, Okay.

He sets his oxygen tank aside, leans it against the wall, and picks up his backpack. I help him sling it onto his shoulder. No machete, no weaponry. He's wearing his skinny blue shirt, old jeans.

He steps down the stairs, two feet on each step, one step at a time. It takes a long time for him to reach the yard.

He doesn't look back.

My father walks across the grass, slow, slow, and he follows the tractor path into the weedfield, down to the swamp. I watch from the porch. He doesn't turn around, he doesn't look back. Near the water, he leans and picks a couple of stalks, maybe loosestrife, it snaps off easy. He circles along the edge of the water and finally up the hill where the path goes into hawthorn trees. Beyond that, he's a brushstroke of blue, moving along the old hay field towards the woods.

I know where he's going. In a minute the path will slope down a bit, he'll be out of sight, with the flat rock ahead, his campsite. He'll sit down, or lie down, with the pines and the fallen-down wild grapevines behind him, a windbreak.

He's on the downslope of the path. I see the back of his head, such a slight gray. I see his shoulders, a scrap of sky.

———————————————

My knees give out. I sink onto the step.

I look out through air. I can see through it. That's what thought is, this climate. Over my father's head. Enveloped, buoyed with winds and atomic streams, a scattering of flesh and word, the dispersal of matter.

How can I stand up and walk into the house?

———————————————

I don't. I stay put.

If my father can sit outside for three days, I can sit here, too.

———————

I think I can smell the path that he took. I close my eyes and I can smell the bent grass, the dirt kicked up where his shoe scraped a stone. There's the mud and the burr-sedge, the fishsmell at the water's edge.

Irene would say I'd lost my senses. But what about this mushroom smell from the right, and the scent of duckweed on the left? If you don't do a thing, it's like dreaming—the world cracks open.

Looking around, I know where animals are, I can see all the blackbirds shifting on weeds, one foot, the other foot, their small adjustments of wings. Canary grass waffles where a muskrat walks. Beside my hand, a phantom-gnat hits the floor of the porch and walks in the direction of shade.

Everything is ongoing. A couple of clouds move west to east and break apart over the silo, they splay out, they recoup. The clouds are white with gray wash bellies, and there, a pheasant croaks out its call and thrums, right there where the wild grapes shake slightly.

———————

When you wake from a dream of a blue dish or a dream of a piece of paper, that's it, you know the loss of the senses. In the dream of the blue dish, my eyesight is perfect, miraculous, and so far beyond 20/20 that the bedroom walls are blurs now, my hands ill-defined, and I think, I *saw* that blue dish. I held it and I could see it! In its entirety: the sheen, the base, the bowl, the curvatures and hollows, the flecks in the blueness, the wholeness of parts, the perfection of flaws.

———————————————

The sun pours down on the floorboards, and I lean back against the brick wall of the house. I take off my boots and my socks, roll up my jeans, and then I twist my T-shirt sleeves into rolls on my shoulders. The sun hits my skin and presses there where the shoulder bones hurt.

The sun is nameless, like the moon. The sun. The moon. Male or female in one tongue or another.

It is easy to see how violence is, in a moment, overwhelmed, transformed, enmeshed. Light touches the body. Holds, holds.

I open and close my eyes.

It's easy to see how full the world is, webbed and replete. Whole.

I won't lift a hand for a while, won't add or subtract a thing.

My father is basking, too.

———————————————

When the sun sets, Irene pounds at the front door. Then she walks around the corner of the house. "Where's your father?" she asks.

He's camping out.

"Overnight?"

He wants to be outside.

"Well, he could be outside here with us," she says.

He wants to be by himself.

"Oh."

She sits down on the floor of the porch beside me, and I pull his note from my pocket and hand it to her. She shakes her head. "No," she says. "No good-bye at all?"

He's been at it for a year, I say.

"I know. I know." She draws her knees up to her chin and hugs her legs. "I just wanted to kiss his hair, that's all."

We stare into the yard.

"Should we go find him?" she asks.

He said to wait three days.

"Where is he?"

We're not going. We'll wait three days, and then we'll find him.

Irene shakes her head again. "How can you do it?" She takes my arm and sets it on her knees. Her hair curtains forward until it covers her face.

Irene says, "He wouldn't want you to sit outside all night."

He's doing what he wants, and I'm doing what I want.

It's dark and the frogs call loud, in choruses, amphitheatered. Even with clouds, the swamp is a visible shape, light gray, cut-out aluminum. Irene leans closer to whisper, like somebody at a concert.

"So he's out that way, out towards the woods?"

We're not going!

"I told him I'd help, I told him that. So, all right. There is *nobody* else I would do this for," Irene says. She stands up and walks to the porch railing. "We'll wait three days—this is already one, right? But I won't wait out here. I'll keep *you* alive for three days! Do you want some coffee? Do you want some pretzels?"

She brings me a pillow and a blanket before she goes inside to sleep on the sofa.

On the beach at the Black Sea, Stalin could not sit down and look at the water. He had his sports. The beach ball. The game of shark. Svetlana on his shoulders, his hands gripping her ankles until he decided to throw her over. Dunking her. Again and again like so many baptisms until she sputtered and stopped laughing.

He walked out of the water and filled his large lungs with air.

Every time he puffed himself up, he thought, Thank god I do not have breasts. If I had breasts, I would cut them off.

On the second day, Irene hooks up her laptop in the kitchen. She takes over the place, brings me coffee and cereal, a toothbrush and a cup of water to spit, a trowel and some toilet paper. I walk out of the yard into the high weeds, but that's as far as I go.

On the porch, I listen. I try to hear my father's breathing. Nothing. Some breezes and whooshing of grasses.

Irene makes too much noise. She opens and closes cupboard doors, asks where the flour is, opens and shuts drawers. She bakes bread. Through the screen door, she talks to me, reads what she writes to Timothy in the chat room. Later, she watches the noon news and the weather and calls out reports on that. Warm, humid, slight chance of showers overnight.

The night of the second day we pile some branches in the back yard, roll up newspaper for kindling, and light a bonfire. Irene rolls potatoes in foil and throws them into the middle of it all.

If my father is still alive, he'll see the light in the sky over the hill. He'll smell the wood smoke, and he'll know we're out here, watching the air over his head, knowing it's that column of sky he is breathing.

If he is dead, the smoke will drift his way like incense and some of the burned dust will fall down on him.

Dust will fall down on him.

On the third day, we eat one of the three-seed loaves Irene baked. The sun hits hard, early, as soon as it breaks above the trees, and the porch floorboards heat up under my feet. Irene splits the loaf and toasts it and brings it out on a plate with butter and sour cherry jam. She fills a big Thermos with coffee and sets everything on the bench. She brings me clean socks and my hiking boots.

"Let's finish the coffee first," she says.

We lean back and watch the field. We listen. Few noises at first, then the day warms and sounds settle into patterns. Song bits. House finches in the arbor vitae. A robin, a kingbird. A flicker on the metal shed roof, hammering. Then it croaks and takes off into the sycamore. As the heat builds, flies crawl up from the ground, climb the grass until their wings dry, and then hang in low clusters, buzzing. By mid-morning the whole yard hums and the fly smell— old muslin, foot dust—blows towards us, up to the porch.

We drink the coffee, and then Irene says, "You set?"

Okay. I won't take anything along. We'll call somebody when we get back.

But Irene wants to take the gun, and I say, Sure. He said you could shoot him when he was dead.

"No!" she says. She opens her mouth wide. "Do you think I should?" She leans on the gun like a cane. She doubles over, and I think she's crying.

You could, I said.

She stands up. She's wearing a purple silk scarf and a satin shirt, and her shoulders are both wet now. She's lined her eyes more dramatically than usual, with thick mascara on her lashes, and all that is smearing into shadows on her face.

I pull on the clean socks and boots. My arms smell like the back yard, part sun, part fly-must, and I tie my boots up slowly.

Irene slings the gun on her shoulder, and we walk down the steps into the back yard.

Flies lift from the grass, collide with our boots, and careen off in waves. The air is jittery up to our knees, and some of the flies buffet onto our arms, those hair legs and wings touching in random hits and falls. Irene pushes the gun like an oar through them until we reach the tractor path in the weeds.

There, we're in the clear. The path is hard-packed and we follow it down to the swamp and around the water, both of us slowing down when we get to the hill. The last steps over it, we know what we'll see ahead. The flat rock. The windbreak of pines and grapevines.

No vultures. A shape like my father's, there, and strewn.

When we are close enough to smell the rot, we stop. Irene stretches out her scarf and hands me one end of it. Covering our mouths and our noses, we walk closer, bend down. Not fit to breathe the same air.

He's done it. He's lured things to him.

He lies on his back, one arm thrown sideways, an odd angle at the shoulder. His shirt is in pieces, fallen to the side, the way the hair of a deer drifts back from the skeleton when something feeds on the muscle.

My father's skin is dried, and what flesh he had on his arms, the sides of his belly, is opened up. And here are the flies again, funneled down on him.

"He must have died right away," Irene says.

She steps closer and, using the gun like a hoe, she scrapes at the ground near my father's arm and pulls his sketchbook towards her feet.

He won't bite, I say.

"I didn't want to disturb him," she says.

Nothing disturbs him. Look at that.

An enormous carrion beetle walks out of his side and steps onto a leaf.

Irene reels around. "I could shoot that beetle!" she says.

And she shoulders the gun, aims at the leaf, and fires.

The blast lifts a cloud of leaves, blows it apart into leaf dust that rains down in bits on my father's side. Everything on the ground recoils, jolted by shock waves. The hair on my father's head moves, and a gray strand detaches, slips away from his scalp. The flies buzz at a higher pitch and swirl; the maggots that had looked like gauze patches on my father's neck twist and put one piece of his skin into a slow motion.

Somebody might hear that, I say.

"It's all right," Irene says. "I just shot at a beetle. I probably missed."

She picks up the sketchbook and looks through it. "He had time to draw," she says, and opens the pages to show me. "Can I keep this?"

It's yours, I say. He gave me his box of leaves.

Something has chewed at my father's mouth. His lips are gone, and his head is pulled sharply down on his shoulder. His teeth are exposed, he is gap-toothed, gaping. On the ground beside him I see his porcelain tooth. Maybe he took it out before he died. The wire clasp is clean, and I pick it up.

Bending that close to my father's face, I can see how far he has already gone. His body is lavish with new colors, metamorphosed into more permanence—his skin so tight to the bone on his wrist it shines metallic. His shoulders are the color of leaf.

My father has dark bowls for eyes now, so much could be swimming in them. His neck and his belly have bloated and fallen, like tents, dropped. He is black and blue, an iridescence on him wherever the sun hits.

"I wouldn't know him," Irene says, "except for the shoes."

Look at his hair, I say. Look at his teeth.

"Look at the shoes on his feet," Irene says.

I know my father.

When they ask, I'll say, yes, I can identify him. He's just who he said he was.

Weathered bits, shreds, an arrangement of bones. Visited, feasted, all gone to pieces, enough for a body bag, plenty to burn.

Look at the flies, the commotion, the turn he has taken. There's the blue of his thumbs, and his jeans, torn, the leaves fallen on him, eruptions of larvae, flies at his fly. His gall bladder set beside him like jade; vultures won't eat it, coyotes won't eat it.

That's him. That's my father.

He's himself, not emptied of anything. His blood the color of dirt, undrinkable. The hands he has washed himself of, there in the leaves.

photo by Dick Schwarz

Janet Kauffman was born in Lancaster, Pennsylvania, and raised on a tobacco farm. She has published several collections of short stories, including *Characters on the Loose* (Graywolf Press), *Obscene Gestures for Women* (Alfred A. Knopf), and *Places in the World a Woman Could Walk* (Alfred A. Knopf). Her short novels, *Collaborators* (Alfred A. Knopf), *The Body in Four Parts* (Graywolf Press), and this book, *Rot*, complete the trilogy *Flesh Made Word*. She teaches at Eastern Michigan University.

New Issues Poetry & Prose

Editor, Herbert Scott

James Armstrong, *Monument in a Summer Hat*
Michael Burkard, *Pennsylvania Collection Agency*
Anthony Butts, *Fifth Season*
Gladys Cardiff, *A Bare Unpainted Table*
Lisa Fishman, *The Deep Heart's Core Is a Suitcase*
Joseph Featherstone, *Brace's Cove*
Robert Grunst, *The Smallest Bird in North America*
Mark Halperin, *Time as Distance*
Myronn Hardy, *Approaching the Center*
Edward Haworth Hoeppner, *Rain Through High Windows*
Janet Kauffman, *Rot* (fiction)
Josie Kearns, *New Numbers*
Maurice Kilwein Guevara, *Autobiography of So-and-so:
    Poems in Prose*
Lance Larsen, *Erasable Walls*
David Dodd Lee, *Downsides of Fish Culture*
Deanne Lundin, *The Ginseng Hunter's Notebook*
Joy Manesiotis, *They Sing to Her Bones*
David Marlatt, *A Hog Slaughtering Woman*
Paula McLain, *Less of Her*
Malena Mörling, *Ocean Avenue*
Julie Moulds, *The Woman with a Cubed Head*
Marsha de la O, *Black Hope*
C. Mikal Oness, *Water Becomes Bone*
Elizabeth Powell, *The Republic of Self*
Margaret Rabb, *Granite Dives*
Rebecca Reynolds, *Daughter of the Hangnail*
Martha Rhodes, *Perfect Disappearance*
John Rybicki, *Traveling at High Speeds*
Mark Scott, *Tactile Values*